P9-DMC-196

Amos Binder,
Secret Agent

DISCARDED

WAYNE PUBLIC LIBRARY WAYNE, NJ

AUG 4 1997

OTHER YEARLING BOOKS YOU WILL ENJOY:

HARRIS AND ME, *Gary Paulsen*
THE HAYMEADOW, *Gary Paulsen*
THE COOKCAMP, *Gary Paulsen*
THE VOYAGE OF THE *FROG, Gary Paulsen*
THE BOY WHO OWNED THE SCHOOL, *Gary Paulsen*
THE RIVER, *Gary Paulsen*
THE MONUMENT, *Gary Paulsen*
THE WINTER ROOM, *Gary Paulsen*
HOW TO EAT FRIED WORMS, *Thomas Rockwell*
HOW TO FIGHT A GIRL, *Thomas Rockwell*

YEARLING BOOKS are designed especially to entertain and enlighten young people. Patricia Reilly Giff, consultant to this series, received her bachelor's degree from Marymount College and a master's degree in history from St. John's University. She holds a Professional Diploma in Reading and a Doctorate of Humane Letters from Hofstra University. She was a teacher and reading consultant for many years, and is the author of numerous books for young readers.

For a complete listing of all Yearling titles, write to Dell Readers Service, P.O. Box 1045, South Holland, IL 60473.

Gary Paulsen

Amos Binder, Secret Agent

CULPEPPER ADVENTURES

A YEARLING BOOK

Published by
Bantam Doubleday Dell Books for Young Readers
a division of
Bantam Doubleday Dell Publishing Group, Inc.
1540 Broadway
New York, New York 10036

If you purchased this book without a cover you should be aware that this book is stolen property. It was reported as "unsold and destroyed" to the publisher and neither the author nor the publisher has received any payment for this "stripped book."

Copyright © 1997 by Gary Paulsen

All rights reserved. No part of this book may be reproduced or transmitted in any form or by any means, electronic or mechanical, including photocopying, recording, or by any information storage and retrieval system, without the written permission of the Publisher, except where permitted by law.

The trademarks Yearling® and Dell® are registered in the U.S. Patent and Trademark Office and in other countries.

ISBN: 0-440-41050-9

Printed in the United States of America

January 1997

10 9 8 7 6 5 4 3 2 1

OPM

Amos Binder, Secret Agent

Chapter · 1

Duncan—Dunc—Culpepper had his dad's video camera trained on his best friend for life, Amos Binder. Amos was watching television. He had been staring at the screen nonstop for thirty-two hours, fifty-seven minutes, and eleven seconds.

"Three more minutes, Amos, and you'll have the world's record. You'll be famous. I left a message with a reporter down at the *Globe*. She said she'd get back to me." Dunc inched around the overstuffed chair to get a shot of Amos's profile from the other side. "Aren't you excited?"

Amos nodded dully. "Ecstatic." His face

1

was puffy and one eye was trying to close on him.

"Two minutes, Amos. A minute and a half . . ."

The telephone rang.

Amos was out of the chair before Dunc could blink.

Dunc hadn't counted on the telephone. It was Amos's greatest weakness. Amos spent his life waiting for a call from a girl named Melissa Hansen. To him Melissa was the most perfect female on the planet and he worshiped her—from a distance. To Melissa, Amos was about as important as a dust ball under the bed. She ignored him completely.

Amos had the strange idea that if Melissa did call, she'd want him to answer on that all-important first ring. As a result, sometimes his body was in motion before his brain kicked in.

This was one of those times.

Amos forgot about the root beer in his left hand and the bowl of cheese puffs on his lap. They crashed to the floor on his first jump. He also forgot about the dozen or so electrical cords plugged into the photographic lights that Dunc had set up around the room.

Amos cleared the first cord, but the second one was knee-high and waiting for him. He hit it full speed, tripped, and pulled over his mother's antique ceramic lamp. It smashed on the corner of the end table.

He tried to catch his balance, wobbled, and rolled into the next string of cords. The telephone had finished its first ring and was starting its second. Amos was desperate. He made a valiant effort to stand up. By now cords were wrapped around his entire body. He stepped forward but the cords snapped him back, seat first, into his mother's rubber tree plant.

Dunc taped the whole thing.

Amos's older sister, Amy, strolled in from the kitchen. She popped her gum and looked over at Amos, who was sitting in the plant with a mass of tangled electrical wires hanging off him. She rolled her eyes and shook her head in disgust.

3

Amos struggled to pry his rear out of the plant holder. "Did you get the phone, Amy? *Amy?*"

Amy rolled her eyes again. "I told Mom and Dad we should have moved away while you were at camp. It was the perfect opportunity. But would they listen to me? No-oo-o." She turned and headed back into the kitchen. At the door she stopped. "By the way, some reporter called. She said to tell you two goon-heads she wasn't going to be able to make it."

Chapter·2

Amos reached into the Binders' mailbox and pulled out a stack of letters. He was sorting through them when he heard someone call his name. He turned and dropped a couple of the letters on the porch.

Dunc was pedaling up the sidewalk waving something. "I've got it figured out, Amos. Don't worry, we're still going to be rich."

Amos ignored him and picked up a large manila envelope addressed to Mr. A. Bender with an official-looking government seal and no return address. He scratched his head. "That's odd. Somebody got my name wrong." He tore off the top and looked in.

Dunc carefully parked his bike and jumped onto the porch. "You've got to see this, Amos." He held up a videotape. "It's great. It's you trying to get to the phone yesterday. If we send it to one of those funny home video shows we're a cinch to win."

"Airplane tickets?" Amos wrinkled his nose. "Now who do you suppose would be sending me round-trip tickets to a place called . . ." He pulled out a letter and unfolded it. "Denison Falls, Arizona?"

Dunc forgot the video and read the letter over Amos's shoulder. "It's signed 'Cyrano.' I didn't know you knew anybody named Cyrano."

"I don't. He says my escort and I should meet him at the airport in Denison Falls and he'll explain everything."

Dunc grabbed the letter and read out loud:

Dear A.B.,
Once again, your government has need of your special talents. Bring your escort

6

and meet me at gate thirty-seven and I will explain your assignment. Your code name is Popeye. Guard the key with your life. If for some reason I am detained, proceed to the Claymore Hotel on Broad Street.

Cyrano

Amos fished around in the envelope and pulled out a gold key. "Here it is. I wonder what it goes to?"

Dunc sat down on the edge of the porch. He looked at the envelope and then back at the letter. "We have a problem here, Amos. Someone thinks you're this A. Bender and they're counting on you to get this key to Arizona."

"Well, that's tough. I can't go to Arizona. My parents grounded me for ten years because of the mess we made in the living room. Besides, my cousin Little Brucie is coming to visit for spring break, and my mom says I'm stuck watching the little monster."

Dunc rubbed his chin.

Amos saw a familiar gleam in his

friend's eyes. He held up his hand. "I know that look, and you can count me out right now. We should take this letter back to the post office and let them handle it."

"You're probably right, Amos." Dunc sighed a long, sorrowful, noisy sigh. "After all, you *are* grounded and I know how much you love baby-sitting your cousin."

"Wait, I never said—"

"And it probably wouldn't be right to tell our folks some big story like . . . we've won a free trip to Denison Falls for spring break and the *key* to the city." Dunc stood up and brushed off his jeans. "No, even if the government needs you because the security of our country is at stake, I guess it just wouldn't be right."

Amos thought about it. "I suppose Amy could watch Little Brucie."

Dunc waited.

"And I'm really not all that anxious to be around when my uncle Alfred gets here and takes off his shoes and picks his toes through his smelly socks."

Dunc waited.

"After all, it is for our country and everything. Okay, I'm in. When do we leave?"

Dunc smiled. "Just as soon as we can convince your parents to un-ground you."

Chapter · 3

"Did you have to wear that?"

Amos tightened the belt of his white trench coat and straightened his dark glasses. "What's the matter with it? I am supposed to be some sort of secret agent, aren't I?"

"I don't think they want you to advertise."

Amos pulled off his glasses and glanced around the busy airport. "I'm not sure it matters. It doesn't look like this Cyrano guy is gonna show, anyway. We've been waiting here at gate thirty-seven for almost an hour. I'm getting hungry."

Just then, a short man with jet-black hair and beady eyes walked furtively across the lobby and sat in the chair beside them. He was wearing a designer suit. "Do you have it?" he whispered.

The two boys looked at each other. Amos slid his dark glasses on. "I'll handle this." He turned to the man. "What's the password?"

The man's face turned ugly. "Don't play games with me, kid. Either you have it or you don't."

Amos glanced back at Dunc and shrugged. "Do we have it?"

"Look, mister." Dunc stood up. "We just got here. Give us a chance to do some sightseeing, maybe get a bite to eat, some rest—"

"Rest! Why, you . . ." The man leaped up and grabbed the front of Dunc's shirt.

"Is everything all right here?" A tall security guard with a long crooked nose was suddenly standing behind them.

The man with the beady eyes dropped his hand. "Quite all right, Officer. I must have mistaken these nice boys for some other boys." He stepped away and walked quickly down the corridor.

The officer smiled. "Seems like we get our share of weirdos around here. Can I get you guys a cab?"

"That'd be great," Dunc said. "We're staying at the Claymore Hotel."

The officer led them to the front of the airport and helped them put their luggage in the trunk of a yellow cab.

Dunc got in the back next to Amos and was about to thank the officer for his trouble when the security guard opened the front door and slid in beside the driver.

Amos whistled. "Wow. I'd say you're really going beyond the call of duty."

The officer turned in the seat. "Name's Cyrano. Which one of you is Popeye?"

"Uh, him." Dunc jerked his thumb toward Amos. "I'm the escort."

"I expected someone a little older for the escort. Oh well, I guess the brass knows what it's doing. Sorry about the wait back there, but I was hoping the other side would tip their hand."

"Did they?" Amos asked.

Cyrano nodded. "That unpleasant fellow back at the airport was Beltron. We have a file on him two inches thick. He works for whoever pays the most and he usually doesn't care what the job is. Did he ask you for the key?"

Amos asked, "What do you mean, he doesn't care what the job is?"

Dunc ignored Amos. "Beltron didn't exactly ask for the key. He wanted to know if we had *it*."

"Whatever you do, don't let that key fall into the wrong hands," Cyrano said.

"I've got it right here." Amos patted his foot. "I figured it would be safe inside my sock. Although"—he frowned—"it is starting to make a big blister and . . ."

The tall man pulled a folder out of the glove compartment. "We don't have a lot of time for your briefing so here's the case in a nutshell. There are some high-ranking foreign officials from the Middle East visiting our country. One of the ambassadors brought his daughter along and they're staying at the Claymore. Because of your martial arts skills and your age the brass thought you'd be the perfect inside man."

"Absolutely right," said Amos, puffing out his chest. He leaned over to Dunc and whispered, "What's an inside man?"

The cab pulled up in front of an enormous hotel. Cyrano jumped out and retrieved their bags from the trunk. He handed Amos the folder. "Read this. You and your escort are in room one thirty-four. I'll check back with you later. Good luck." The big man stepped back into the cab and it sped away.

"Correct me if I'm wrong"—Amos looked up at the fifteen-story hotel—"but did I hear him say that I know martial arts?"

"That's what it sounded like."

Amos picked up his bag. "I have the strangest feeling that you've gotten me in trouble again."

Chapter·4

Amos flipped a switch on the wall. "This room has everything. Even electric curtains." He watched the drapes swing back and forth.

"Quit playing around, Amos. This is important." Dunc had the contents of the folder spread out on the floor around him. "This girl you're supposed to meet is the granddaughter of a sheik. Her name is Fatima Khalil. Your job is to get her to trust you and then report everything she says back to Cyrano. Look, they gave us two invitations for a big party in her honor down in the ballroom tonight."

Amos made a flying leap for the middle of the king-sized bed. He settled back against the pillows. "This is the life. I'm going to call Room Service. You want anything?"

"Order me a cheeseburger." Dunc studied one of the reports. "It says here that Fatima travels with over a million dollars in jewels."

Amos put the phone down. "Room Service said they'd be right up with the food." He picked up the remote control. "Maybe the ambassador's daughter will decide she likes us and force us to take a couple of thousand in diamonds off her hands."

Before Amos could turn the television on, there was a loud knock on the door.

"That was fast." Amos slid off the bed and went to the door.

When he opened it a pretty young girl with brown eyes and long dark hair rushed into the room. She clutched Amos's arm. "Please, you have to help me. Someone is following me."

Dunc came out of the bedroom carrying

the folder. When he saw the girl, he shoved it behind his back. "What's going on?"

The girl fell to the couch exhausted. "I'm so sorry to have bothered you like this but I didn't know what else to do. A man stopped me in the elevator and tried to take my necklace." She fingered a diamond chain around her neck. "When the elevator stopped I managed to get away and I ran to the first room I came to. I think he's still after me."

Dunc went to the door and cautiously peeked out. There was no one in sight. "All clear." He shut the door. "Do you want us to call the police for you?"

"No!" The girl jumped up. "That would cause international problems. You see, my father is a goodwill ambassador to your country."

"Hey, that's a coincidence." Amos chewed on a fingernail. "We were just— Ouch!"

Dunc had stomped on the toe of Amos's tennis shoe. "What my friend means is we were just about to explore the hotel and

we'd be happy to walk you to your room,"
Dunc said.

"How kind of you." The girl fluttered her
long eyelashes at Dunc. "Our entourage is
staying in the penthouse. You must meet
my father. I'm sure he will want to reward
you for your compassion."

Dunc slid the folder under the nearest
chair cushion and opened the door. The
hallway was still empty. "Amos, you check
the elevator and I'll bring Ms. . . ." He
turned to the girl. "What was your name?"

"You may call me Fatima." She winked
and flashed him a brilliant smile. "What's
yours?"

A light shade of pink spread over Dunc's
face. "Duncan. Dunc for short."

"Hurrummmp." Amos cleared his throat.
"In case anyone is interested, my name is
Amos and I really hate to break this up, but
can we hurry? My food is due here in a few
minutes . . ."

"Right." Dunc blinked as if to clear his
thoughts. "Go ahead, Amos. We're right behind you."

Chapter · 5

The elevator opened and Fatima led them to the door of the penthouse. She put her card in the key slot and the door opened.

The boys followed her inside and were instantly grabbed from behind and slammed up against the wall.

"Enough!" Fatima clapped her hands and the boys were dropped to the floor.

Amos rubbed his throat. Their attackers were two large men with bulging muscles. They were standing guard like pit bulls on either side of the door.

"Don't let Riyah and Hejaz bother you,"

Fatima laughed. "They're pretty much harmless."

"Sure." Amos moved behind her. "Sort of the same way a crazed grizzly bear in a salmon stream is harmless, right?"

Fatima laughed again. "They are my father's bodyguards. They won't hurt you unless they have orders."

An elderly woman with wrinkled skin and a stooped back hobbled into the room. Fatima took off her necklace and handed it to her. "Put this in the safe, Mesha. Someone tried to relieve me of it today."

The woman didn't comment. She reached inside her shirt collar and pulled out a chain with a gold key on the end.

Dunc's eyes bugged out. The key looked identical to the one Amos had hidden inside his sock. He watched the old woman kneel beside the fireplace and put the key in what appeared to be an electrical outlet. A secret panel popped open. She placed the necklace inside a black case and closed the door.

"Mesha, make our guests comfortable while I speak to my father," Fatima ordered. She turned to Dunc and smiled sweetly. "Make yourself at home, Duncan. I'll be right back."

Mesha motioned for the boys to follow her into the kitchen. She brought two tall drinks to the table and silently left the room.

"And I thought *our* room was great. Did you see that aquarium in the living room? You could swim in that thing." Amos picked up one of the drinks and took a sip.

"Did you get a look at the key?" Dunc whispered.

"What key?"

"The one the old woman used to open the safe."

"What about it?"

"It's identical to yours."

Amos looked puzzled. "Why would the government give us a key to Fatima's safe?"

Dunc shrugged. "I don't know. That part wasn't in the folder."

Mesha appeared in the door of the kitchen and motioned for them to come with her. Amos put his glass on the table and they followed her back to the living room.

Fatima was standing next to a distinguished-looking man with a short gray beard. "These are the boys I told you about, Father."

The man stepped forward and eagerly reached to shake their hands. "Words cannot thank you enough for what you have done. Please let me express my gratitude by repaying you in some way."

"What did you have in mind?" Amos casually leaned one elbow against the six-foot-long aquarium.

"Name your price. Fatima is my only daughter. Her safety is invaluable."

Dunc coughed. "He was just kidding, sir. We don't need a reward. We were glad to help. Weren't we, Amos?"

The aquarium started to move. One of the guards ran over to steady it just as it started to topple off its pedestal. Water sloshed out, drenching the guard and soaking the carpet.

Dunc grabbed Amos's sleeve and dragged him toward the door. "It was really nice meeting all of you, but I just remembered we have an appointment."

Fatima followed them. "It's a shame you

have to leave so soon. But now that you know where I'm staying, Duncan, please don't be a stranger."

"Don't worry." Amos jerked his arm away. "I'm sure *Duncan* will be back."

Chapter · 6

They had barely made it back to their room when there was another knock on the door.

"Room Service."

Amos vaulted over the couch and raced to the door. "Food. Thank goodness. I think I was starting to get faint."

The waiter pushed a small serving cart into the center of the living room. Amos was so busy taking the lids off the dishes that he didn't notice when the waiter quietly closed the door.

Cyrano laughed at him. "Man, you must really be hungry."

Amos glanced up. Between mouthfuls he mumbled, "Boy, you sure do get around. One minute you're a police officer, the next you're a waiter."

"In our line of work a person has to be flexible." Cyrano smiled. "But then I guess you know all about that."

Dunc picked up his cheeseburger. "We didn't think you would contact us this soon."

"I had word that you and Popeye have already managed to get inside the ambassador's suite. I'm impressed at how quickly you guys work. What did you find out?"

"Not much." Dunc took a bite of the cheeseburger. "The ambassador's daughter had a run-in with a jewel thief. We walked her to the penthouse and her dad thanked us. That's about it."

Cyrano frowned and shook his head. "We were afraid something like this might happen. The government tried to talk Ambassador Khalil into leaving his daughter's jewelry at home but it was no go. He said it was a matter of custom. In his country his daughter is of marriageable age and no female looking for a husband would be seen without her dowry." ·

Amos dug his elbow into Dunc's side. "So, she's looking for a husband—*Duncan.*"

Dunc ignored him. "Do you have some sort of plan to protect the jewels?"

"It just so happens . . ." Cyrano reached under the white cloth covering the cart and pulled out a small black case. He flipped it open. Inside was an assortment of jeweled necklaces, rings, earrings, and bracelets. "We do."

"Whoa! We could retire on this. I could buy Melissa a summer home in the mountains and play video games till I die." Amos ran his fingers through the jewelry.

"Not exactly." Cyrano closed the case and handed it to Amos. "These are all fakes."

"I don't get it." Amos made a face. "Why would we want fakes?"

"Because they want us to substitute the fake jewels for the real ones in Khalil's safe." Dunc sat on the couch. "Isn't that right, Cyrano?"

"The brass thinks it's best to be cautious. That way if anything does get stolen, nothing of value is really lost."

Amos scratched his head. "And just how are we supposed to make the switch? Khalil's suite is full of people, not to mention those two trained gorillas who stand guard by the door."

"The brass wants you to handle it delicately. Khalil must never know about the fakes. He would be offended." Cyrano pushed the cart toward the door. He tossed a small packet on the couch. "These might come in handy."

Dunc closed the door behind Cyrano. "What did he give you?"

"The label says 'knockout pills.'" Amos wolfed down the last of his burger. "I don't know about you, but I vote we give Cyrano the key to the safe and let him handle it from here. In fact I was thinking maybe it was time for us to call it quits and go home. Melissa's probably wondering where I am by now."

Dunc closed his eyes. He thought about telling Amos that Melissa Hansen couldn't care less where he was—ever. Instead he decided to try to convince Amos to stay until they made some progress in the case. Dunc wanted to read the file again. He felt under the chair cushion.

The folder was gone.

Chapter·7

Amos splashed more water on his hair. One long piece in the back refused to lie flat. "You're not fooling me a bit. I know the real reason you talked me into going to this dance."

"Like I said, we have to go to the party to keep an eye on Fatima's jewelry and to watch for an opportunity to get back inside the ambassador's suite." Dunc straightened his tie and checked his teeth in the bathroom mirror. He brushed an imaginary piece of lint off his sleeve.

"You've obviously forgotten who you're

talking to here," Amos said. "If anybody knows the signs, it's me."

"Signs of what?"

"Romance, true love. You've got it bad."

"Don't be dumb. All I want to do is finish this case and go home."

"Whatever you say—*Duncan.*"

"Get real, Amos. There are a lot of strange things going on here and I just don't want to leave them hanging. Are you ready?"

"Right behind you, Romeo."

"Cut that out. Did you remember to hide the fake jewels?"

"Hidden."

"How about the knockout pills?"

Amos patted his pocket. "Got 'em right here."

"Then let's go. I don't want to be late."

"I bet you don't." Amos followed him to the elevator. "Maybe Melissa will agree to a double wedding. We'll let Fatima's dad pick up the tab."

Dunc pushed the button for the first floor. "Now, remember. You're supposed to be a hotshot secret agent working on an important case. Mingle with the guests, but keep your eyes open for anything suspicious."

"Whatever you say, loverboy." Amos started whistling the wedding march.

When the doors opened in the lobby Dunc stopped a bellboy to ask directions to the ballroom. The freckle-faced young man smiled and pointed to the right.

Music drifted out the double doors. A band was set up at the far end of the room, and off to one side was a buffet table heaped with every kind of food imaginable.

"Hey, this is my kind of party." Amos licked his lips and started for the buffet.

Dunc was about to follow when he spotted Fatima. A diamond tiara sparkled in her hair and she wore a matching pendant around her neck.

She saw him at the same time. "Duncan! I'm so happy to see you. No one told me you were coming. Where's your friend?"

Dunc pointed at the buffet table. Amos already had one plate loaded and was trying to manage a second. "Looks like we better get something to eat before he takes it all."

"Actually," Fatima said, smiling, "I was wondering if we could dance."

"Dance?" Dunc cleared his throat and loosened his collar. "It seems kinda hot for dancing."

A waitress tapped Fatima on the shoulder. "There's a telephone call for you, Ms. Khalil. You may take it in the next room. Right this way."

"Will you excuse me, Duncan? Perhaps we can have that dance when I return?"

"No problem." Dunc breathed a sigh of relief. He watched Fatima follow the waitress out of the ballroom.

A short man in a dark suit was standing by a plant near the door. He followed Fatima into the next room.

Amos strolled over to his friend. "Would you mind holding one of these?" He held out a plate. "It's hard to eat without a free hand."

"Hmmm." Dunc rubbed his chin. "There's something familiar about that guy." He snapped his fingers. "Beltron!" he yelled. "Let's go, Beltron is after Fatima!"

Amos shoved his plates at a man wearing a purple sash and a turban. "Take good care of these. I'll be back."

Dunc was already in the next room when Amos caught up with him.

Fatima was on the floor. "It was that man from the elevator. He stole my grandmother's diamond tiara!"

Chapter · 8

Dunc pointed to the lighted display above the elevator doors. "He's headed for the basement, Amos. Come on. We'll take the stairs."

They crashed through the stairwell door and bounded down the stairs two and three at a time until they got to the basement level. They flew through the doors just in time to see the man dash from the elevator.

"There he goes!" Amos spotted a dark pants leg disappearing behind a laundry cart.

Dunc gave the cart a push and sent it flying into Beltron's back. The man stumbled but was on his feet in seconds, heading through a set of swinging doors.

They pushed through the doors and stopped.

Beltron was nowhere in sight.

"What do we do now?" Amos whispered.

Dunc motioned for Amos to go around the left side of a row of washing machines while he took the right.

They met at the end. Dunc shrugged. His voice was low. "He's got to be here somewhere. There's no other way out."

A muffled noise came from somewhere in front of them.

"Look over there by those lockers, Amos, and I'll check these laundry hampers."

"Uh, Dunc. A thought just occurred to me. What exactly are we going to do when we find him?"

Amos realized that he was talking to himself. Dunc was already half buried in a huge hamper and throwing dirty towels out over his head.

Amos moved cautiously around the edge of the lockers. One of them was standing wide open.

"Dunc. You better get over here."

"Did you find him?" Dunc rounded the corner at a run.

"You could say that." Amos moved so that Dunc could see the locker.

Beltron was unconscious. His head and shoulders were in the locker and his legs were sticking out on the floor. The diamond tiara was lying on his stomach.

The swinging doors flew open behind them and footsteps rushed to the lockers.

"Man, I've seen good before, but you guys are something else." Cyrano picked up the tiara and examined it. "Not even dented. Wait till the brass hears about this."

He handed the tiara to Amos. "Maybe you can use it as an excuse to get in Khalil's safe. I'd better disappear before the security guards get down here." The big man vanished out the door before they could stop him.

"He thinks we did this." Amos turned the tiara over in his hand.

"I know." Dunc scratched his head. "The question is, if we didn't—who did?"

Chapter · 9

"I don't think Cyrano wanted you to give that tiara back to Fatima right away." Amos unlocked the door of their room. "Remember, he said maybe we could use it to get in the safe."

"I know what he said." Dunc took off his tie. "But I couldn't let Fatima worry like that. She seemed awfully glad to get it back."

"I'll say. Boy, did she ever plant one on you. Right on the lips too. I thought girls from her country were supposed to be shy."

Dunc's face started to turn pink. "She

was just excited. That was her way of saying she was grateful."

"I sure wouldn't mind if Melissa ever wanted to be grateful." Amos flipped the switch to open the electric curtains. A freckle-faced boy with red hair was sitting on the iron railing of the balcony, grinning.

"Uh . . . Dunc, we have a visitor."

Dunc raised one eyebrow. "That's the bellboy from the lobby."

The boy opened the glass doors and strode into the room. "You guys aren't bad for rank amateurs. A little more polish and they'd probably hire you." He sat down in the wing-back chair.

"Do we know you?" Amos asked.

"No, but you should. You're using my identity."

"So you're A. Bender?" Dunc moved to the couch.

"The one and only Andy Bender. Or so I thought, until now."

"Oh, you still are. I mean, it was all a mistake," Amos said. "You see, I got this letter—"

"We know all about that. Cyrano sent

you that letter. Somehow his people came up with the wrong address. I was in Hong Kong when they contacted me about the situation." Andy took a folder out of his jacket and tossed it on the table.

"So that's where it went." Dunc picked the folder up and thumbed through it. "I never got a chance to finish reading it."

"Sorry about borrowing it. But I had to see what I was supposed to be doing."

Dunc sat down. "You weren't by any chance in the laundry room awhile ago?"

Andy smiled. "I thought I'd save you guys some trouble and take that bozo out for you."

"Then you really do know martial arts?" Amos sat on the arm of the couch and leaned forward. "To tell you the truth, Andy, I'm kinda glad you showed up. This whole thing is getting out of hand. Cyrano wants us to break into Ambassador Khalil's safe and switch fake jewels for the real ones. Now that you're here, you can take over."

"So that's his game." Andy rubbed the back of his neck.

"His game?" Dunc looked worried. "You mean Cyrano isn't one of the good guys?"

Andy sighed. "Maybe I better explain things. Cyrano does work for the government. And in the past he's been one of our very best agents. But lately all kinds of strange stuff has been happening on his cases. Priceless artifacts turned up missing from his mission to Egypt. His partner died mysteriously in South Africa, and a fortune in gold was taken from a museum."

"That doesn't necessarily mean he's guilty, does it?" Amos leaned back. "I mean, those things happen in your line of work."

"True, but when he started this case, the government put a tail on him. They discovered he's very friendly with a known double agent—Beltron."

"Beltron!" Dunc did a double take.

"He's definitely guilty." Amos pounded the back of the couch. "Call your boss and tell him to send someone to come pick him up."

"Unfortunately it's not that simple. We have to catch Cyrano in the act to make sure he stays behind bars."

"Well, I hope it works out for you." Amos stood up. "Let us know what happens."

"Actually, I was hoping you two would stay around and help out. Cyrano has never met me. For all he knows, you really are Popeye. If we keep it that way, I can move around secretly behind the scenes and set a trap for him."

"I'd really like to." Amos pulled his suitcase out of the closet. "But I've got important stuff to do back home. Right, Dunc?"

Dunc was still sitting on the couch. "Maybe we should stay, Amos. After all, we did sort of horn in on Andy's case and mess things up for him."

Amos stared at his friend. "And just whose big idea was that?"

"I know, I convinced you to come. But now that we're here we can't very well back out when Andy really needs us, can we?"

"Why not?"

"Amos!"

"He'll be fine, Dunc. He's a professional."

"Okay, Amos. If you want to go home, I won't try and stop you. Of course there is that other thing."

Amos stopped. "What other thing?"

"Never mind. It's probably not important enough for you to worry about."

"What thing?" Amos's voice had a sharp edge.

"I was thinking about your relationship with Melissa and how it could use a little help."

"So?"

"Well, it's just . . . haven't you noticed how girls really go for the hero type? Look at Fatima."

Amos wavered. "You could have a point."

Andy joined in. "They especially go crazy over secret agents. Being a gentleman and everything, I can't give you details, but take my word for it, they just eat this stuff up."

Amos tapped his fingers on the top of his suitcase. "I suppose it is my patriotic duty to stay and see justice done."

Andy clapped his hands. "All right! Now all we have to do is make a plan to catch a thief."

Chapter · 10

"You call this a plan?" Amos nodded at a cleaning woman and waited until she was gone. "How is one guy going to get rid of a whole suiteful of people?"

"I don't know." Dunc paced the floor outside the Khalil suite. "All I know is Andy said to meet him here at eight o'clock and he'd have everything taken care of for us."

The door to the suite swung open. A hand wearing a black glove gestured for them to enter. They darted inside and closed the door.

Andy, dressed entirely in black and wearing his usual grin, was waiting for them. The two bodyguards were slumped on the floor near the door. Mesha seemed to be sleeping peacefully on the couch.

"How did you do it?" Amos pointed at the guards. "Those guys are three times your size."

"Tricks of the trade." Andy headed toward the balcony window. "And of course those knockout pills you gave me didn't hurt."

"Where's Fatima?" Dunc asked.

"That could prove to be a problem for you." Andy slid the glass door open. "She's out shopping and her father is in a meeting. You'll have to work fast so they don't come in on you. Good luck."

Andy disappeared over the edge of the railing. Amos stared at the empty balcony in awe. "How did he do that?"

Dunc shook his head. "Who knows? Come on, we better make the switch before Fatima and her dad get back. Do you have the key?"

"Right here." Amos pulled off his shoe and sock. "Boy, will I be glad to get rid of this thing. My skin was starting to grow around it."

Dunc took the key and put it into the phony electric outlet. The secret panel popped open. He took out the jewels and handed them to Amos. Then he slid the case with the fakes from under his shirt and placed them in the safe.

"That was a piece of cake, Amos. Let's get the real ones back to our room and wait for Andy."

Amos was watching the fish in the aquarium. One of the larger fish gulped down a small one. "Hey, did you see that? These guys play rough."

"We don't have time to watch the fish, Amos. Let's get out of here."

"I'm right behind you." Amos was still looking at the fish when he started for the door. The toe of his right foot caught in the mouth of the bearskin rug lying on the floor and he shot forward.

Dunc turned just in time to see the jewel case splash into the water and drop to the bottom of the aquarium. "That's just great,

Amos. Reach in there and get it. We're in a little bit of a hurry here."

"I don't think so."

"Why not?"

"I've been watching the fish in there. They have teeth. Sharp teeth."

Dunc bent down. "You're right. Those aren't ordinary fish. They're piranhas, man-eaters."

"So long, jewels. I'm outta here." Amos headed for the door.

"Hang on." Dunc barely caught the back of Amos's shirt. "Maybe we can find something we can use to pull the case out."

Amos glanced around the room. "Nope, I don't see anything. Let's go."

"Hand me Mesha's cane. It's over there by the couch." Dunc pulled a chair up next to the aquarium.

Amos handed him the cane. "Whatever you do, don't get your hand close to the water."

Gingerly Dunc lowered the curved end of the cane into the aquarium. The piranhas circled around it.

One of the guards shifted position.

The boys froze.

The big man muttered something and went back to his snoring.

"Hurry, Dunc," Amos whispered tensely. "I'd almost rather face the fish than those two goons."

"I've just about got it." Dunc inched the case up the side of the glass wall to the top. "Reach in and get it before it falls again, Amos!"

"Are you nuts?"

"It's slipping!"

Amos made a wild grab and scooped the case out onto the floor.

Dunc let out his breath and reached to pick it up. "For a minute there I thought we were gonna lose it, Amos. Amos?"

Amos was holding up his arm. The bottom of his sleeve had a big piece ripped out of it.

They turned to the tank. One of the piranhas was swallowing the last of the material.

Amos's eyes narrowed into tiny slits.

"Now wait a minute, Amos. Let's just try and stay calm."

"When this is over," Amos hissed to Dunc, "if we're both still alive, I'm gonna kill you!"

Chapter · 11

Andy was waiting for them when they got back to their room. "What took you guys so long?"

Amos blew air through his teeth. "It's a long story."

Dunc handed Andy the jewel case and fell into the nearest chair. "Now what?"

"We wait until Cyrano contacts you again. We have agents stationed around the hotel ready to move in when I give the signal."

The telephone rang. Dunc answered it. "Hello." He was quiet for a few seconds. "I understand. . . . Yes, we have them. . . .

All right. . . . We'll meet you in thirty minutes." He hung up the phone.

"Who was it?" Amos asked as he got comfortable on the couch.

"Cyrano's kidnapped Fatima. He's been tipped off. He knows the government is after him and that we have the jewels. He says we have to bring them to the airport or we'll never see her again."

"I'll call my people." Andy jumped up and reached for the phone.

Dunc put his hand on Andy's arm. "He said Popeye and I have to come alone or else."

"Cyrano can be very dangerous." Andy's look was serious. "Are you sure you want it this way?"

Dunc nodded. "He won't hurt anybody if he gets the jewelry."

Andy gave him the case. "I don't like it."

Dunc tucked the jewels under his arm. "Are you coming, Amos?"

Amos chewed on the inside of his cheek. "Maybe we could call in a SWAT team. How about the National Guard? They have experience with this sort of thing."

"We're running out of time." Dunc headed out the door.

"I hate it when he does that." Amos went through the door muttering to himself. "He knows I'll follow him. I always follow him. Next time I'll surprise him. . . ."

Chapter · 12

The ride to the airport seemed to take forever. Dunc checked his watch every few seconds. When the cab finally stopped, he threw some money at the driver, jumped out, and raced inside with Amos right behind him.

"Cyrano said to meet him back at gate thirty-seven. We have five minutes."

They pushed and shoved their way through the crowded airport, emptied their pockets for the metal detector, and raced up the escalator.

"There he is, Amos. See that guy in the

last row with the newspaper and the dark glasses? That's Cyrano. Look at him sitting there as cool as a cucumber."

They ran down the aisle and swung over the rail. Amos was gasping for breath.

Dunc trotted into the waiting area and stood in front of Cyrano. He held out the jewel case. "Here they are. Where's Fatima?"

Cyrano opened the case and examined the jewelry. An evil smile spread across his face. He snapped it shut. "I'm really disappointed in the two of you. I had expected you to try something. In fact I was hoping you would. It makes life so interesting."

"You got what you wanted. Tell us where she is."

Cyrano laughed. "I'll phone you her location from South America."

Amos stumbled over a large brown suitcase. Beads of sweat ran down his forehead.

"A little out of shape, aren't we, Popeye? Ha! The two of you are jokes." Cyrano pushed Amos. "Get out of my way."

Amos started to fall backward, but he

braced his legs on the suitcase and managed to stay upright. The suitcase didn't budge.

"She's in the luggage, Amos!" Dunc yelled.

Cyrano glanced anxiously around the waiting area, which was filling up with people. He backed away and tried to melt into the busy crowd.

An elderly woman stuck out her cane and tripped him. Cyrano fell flat on his back. Before he could get up, she flipped him over and snapped a pair of handcuffs on him.

"Mesha?" Fatima crawled out of the unzipped suitcase.

Mesha grinned and tossed the jewel case to a redheaded bystander.

"Andy?" Amos's eyes widened.

"We just happened to be in the neighborhood," Andy joked. "By the way, Mesha is one of us."

"I don't get it," Dunc said. "If she's one of the good guys, why didn't you just have her steal the jewels? It would have saved us a lot of trouble."

"Sorry about that." Andy helped Fatima to her feet. "Cyrano had too many informers at the hotel. We couldn't let him know we had Mesha on the inside."

"Would someone please tell me what is going on here?" Fatima pleaded.

Andy offered her his arm. "I'd be delighted, Ms. Khalil. You see, it's like this . . ." He looked over his shoulder at Dunc and winked. Then he led her down the corridor. "It's a tough job saving lives . . ."

"Are you just going to stand there and watch him steal your woman?" Amos demanded.

Dunc shrugged. "That's the way it goes. You win some, you lose some."

"There's always Bertha Abercromby."

"What?"

"You know. Tall Bertha. She really has a crush on you. When we get back, I'll talk to her. Maybe I can set something up."

"Do me a favor, Amos."

"Name it."

"Don't do me any favors!"

**Be sure to join Dunc and Amos in these
other Culpepper Adventures:**

The Case of the Dirty Bird

When Dunc Culpepper and his best friend,
Amos Binder, first see the parrot in a pet store,
they're not impressed—it's smelly, scruffy, and
missing half its feathers. They're only slightly
impressed when they learn that the parrot
speaks four languages, has outlived ten of its
owners, and is probably 150 years old. But
when the bird starts mouthing off about buried
treasure, Dunc and Amos get pretty excited.
Let the amateur sleuthing begin!

Dunc's Doll

Dunc and his accident-prone friend Amos are
up to their old sleuthing habits once again. This
time they're after a band of doll thieves! When
a doll that once belonged to Charles Dickens's
daughter is stolen from an exhibition at the local mall, the two boys put on their detective

gear and do some serious snooping. Will a vicious watchdog keep them from retrieving the valuable missing doll?

Culpepper's Cannon

Dunc and Amos are researching the Civil War cannon that stands in the town square when they find a note inside telling them about a time portal. Entering it through the dressing room of La Petite, a women's clothing store, the boys find themselves in downtown Chatham on March 8, 1862—the day before the historic clash between the *Monitor* and the *Merrimac*. But the Confederate soldiers they meet mistake them for Yankee spies. Will they make it back to the future in one piece?

Dunc Gets Tweaked

Dunc and Amos meet up with a new buddy named Lash when they enter the radical world of skateboard competition. When somebody "cops"—steals—Lash's prototype skateboard, the boys are determined to get it back. After all, Lash is about to shoot for a totally rad world's record! Along the way they learn a major lesson: *Never* kiss a monkey!

Dunc's Halloween

Dunc and Amos are planning the best route to get the most candy on Halloween. But their plans change when Amos is slightly bitten by a werewolf. He begins scratching himself and chasing UPS trucks—he's become a werepuppy!

Dunc Breaks the Record

Dunc and Amos have a small problem when they try hang gliding—they crash in the wilderness. Luckily, Amos has read a book about a boy who survived in the wilderness for fifty-four days. Too bad Amos doesn't have a hatchet. Things go from bad to worse when a wild man holds the boys captive. Can anything save them now?

Dunc and the Flaming Ghost

Dunc's not afraid of ghosts, although Amos is sure that the old Rambridge house is haunted by the ghost of Blackbeard the Pirate. Then the best friends meet Eddie, a meek man who claims to be impersonating Blackbeard's ghost so that he can live in the house in peace. But if that's true, why are flames shooting from his mouth?

Amos Gets Famous

Deciphering a code they find in a library book, Amos and Dunc stumble onto a burglary ring. The burglars' next target is the home of Melissa, the girl of Amos's dreams (who doesn't even know he's alive). Amos longs to be a hero to Melissa, so nothing will stop him from solving this case—not even a mind-boggling collision with a jock, a chimpanzee, and a toilet.

Dunc and Amos Hit the Big Top

To impress Melissa, Amos decides to perform on the trapeze at the visiting circus. Look out below! But before Dunc can talk him out of his plan, the two stumble across a mystery behind the scenes at the circus. Now Amos is in double trouble. What's really going on under the big top?

Dunc's Dump

Camouflaged as piles of rotting trash, Dunc and Amos are sneaking around the town dump. Dunc wants to find out who is polluting the garbage at the dump with hazardous and toxic waste. Amos just wants to impress Melissa. Can either of them succeed?

Dunc and the Scam Artists

Dunc and Amos are at it again. Some older residents of their town have been bilked by con artists, and the two boys want to look into these crimes. They meet elderly Betsy Dell, whose nasty nephew Frank gives the boys the creeps. Then they notice some soft dirt in Ms. Dell's shed, and a shovel. Does Frank have something horrible in store for Dunc and Amos?

Dunc and Amos and the Red Tattoos

Dunc and Amos head for camp and face two weeks of fresh air—along with regulations, demerits, KP, and inedible food. But where these two best friends go, trouble follows. They overhear a threat against the camp director and discover that camp funds have been stolen. Do these crimes have anything to do with the tattoo of the exotic red flower that some of the camp staff have on their arms?

Dunc's Undercover Christmas

It's Christmastime, and Dunc, Amos, and Amos's cousin T.J. hit the mall for some serious shopping. But when the seasonal magic is threatened by disappearing presents, and Santa Claus himself is a prime suspect, the boys put their celebration on hold and go undercover in perfect Christmas disguises! Can the sleuthing trio protect Santa's threatened reputation and catch the impostor before he strikes again?

The Wild Culpepper Cruise

When Amos wins a "Why I Love My Dog" contest, he and Dunc are off on the Caribbean cruise of their dreams! But there's something downright fishy about Amos's suitcase, and before they know it, the two best friends wind up with more high-seas adventure than they bargained for. Can Dunc and Amos figure out who's out to get them and salvage what's left of their vacation?

Dunc and the Haunted Castle

When Dunc and Amos are invited to spend a week in Scotland, Dunc can already hear the bagpipes a-blowin'. But when the boys spend their first night in an ancient castle, it isn't bagpipes they hear. It's moans! Dunc hears groaning coming from inside his bedroom walls. Amos notices that the eyes of a painting follow him across the room! Could the castle really be haunted? Local legend has it that the castle's former lord wanders the ramparts at night in search of his head! Team up with Dunc and Amos as they go ghostbusting in the Scottish Highlands!

Cowpokes and Desperadoes

Git along, little dogies! Dunc and Amos are bound for Uncle Woody Culpepper's Santa Fe cattle ranch for a week of fun. But when they overhear a couple of cowpokes plotting to do Uncle Woody in, the two sleuths are back on the trail of some serious action! Who's been making off with all the prize cattle? Can Dunc and Amos stop the rustlers in time to save the ranch?

Prince Amos

When their fifth-grade class spends a weekend interning at the state capitol, Dunc and Amos find themselves face-to-face with Amos's walking double—Prince Gustav, Crown Prince of Moldavia! His Royal Highness is desperate to uncover a traitor in his ranks. And when he asks Amos to switch places with him, Dunc holds his breath to see what will happen next. Can Amos pull off the impersonation of a lifetime?

Coach Amos

Amos and Dunc have their hands full when their school principal asks *them* to coach a local T-ball team. For one thing, nobody on the team even knows first base from left field, and the season opener is coming right up. And then there's that sinister-looking gangster driving by in his long black limo and making threats. Can Dunc and Amos fend off screaming tots, ner-

vous mothers, and the mob, and be there when
the ump yells "Play ball"?

Amos and the Alien

When Amos and his best friend, Dunc, have a
close encounter with an extraterrestrial named
Girrk, Dunc thinks they should report their
findings to NASA. But Amos has other plans.
He not only promises to help Girrk find a way
back to his planet, he invites him to hide out
under his bed! Then weird things start to happen—Scruff, the Binders' dog, can't move,
Amos scores a game-winning *touchdown,* and
Dunc knows Girrk is behind Amos's new pow-
ers. What's the mysterious alien really up to?

Dunc and Amos Meet the Slasher

Why is mild-mannered Amos dressed in
leather, slicking back his hair, strutting around
the cafeteria, and going by a phony name?
Could it be because of that new kid, Slasher,
who's promised to eat Amos for lunch? Or has
Amos secretly gone undercover? Amos and his
pal Dunc have some hot leads and are close to

cracking a stolen stereo racket, but Dunc is worried Amos has taken things too far!

Dunc and the Greased Sticks of Doom

Five . . . four . . . three . . . two . . . Olympic superstar Francesco Bartoli is about to hurl himself down the face of a mountain in another attempt to clinch the world slalom speed record. Cheering fans and snapping cameras are everywhere. But someone is out to stop him, and Dunc thinks he knows who it is. Can Dunc get to the gate in time to save the day? Will Amos survive longer than fifteen minutes on the icy slopes? Join best friends Dunc Culpepper and Amos Binder as they take an action-packed winter ski vacation filled with fun, fame, and high-speed high jinks.

Amos's Killer Concert Caper

Amos is desperate. He's desperate for two tickets to the romantic event of his young life—the Road Kill concert! He'll do anything to get them because he heard from a friend of a friend of a friend of Melissa Hansen that she's way into Road Kill. But when he enlists the help of his best friend, Dunc, he winds up with more than he bargained for—backstage, with a mystery to solve. Somebody's trying to make Road Kill live up to its name. Can Dunc and Amos find out who and keep the music playing?

Amos Gets Married

Everybody knows Amos Binder is crazy in love with Melissa Hansen. Only Melissa hasn't given any indication that she even knows Amos exists as a life-form. That is, until now. Suddenly things with Melissa are different. A wave, a wink—an affectionate "snookems"? Can this really be Melissa . . . and *Amos*? Dunc is determined to get to the bottom of it all, but who can blame Amos if his feet don't touch the ground?

Amos Goes Bananas

Amos has more than a monkey on his back. It's a gorilla. Her name is Louise—and she's in love with him. Dunc isn't much help. He's convinced Louise is the key to solving a really big-time case involving some assassins and a respected senator. Who will prevail? Dunc? The assassins? Or Louise?

Dunc and Amos Go to the Dogs

Anyone who knows Amos knows that in his case, dogs are definitely *not* man's best friends. Even his own dog, Scruff, growls and shows his teeth whenever Amos is around. Amos isn't exactly fond of Scruff either. But when Scruff gets mixed up in a dognapping scheme, Amos and Dunc have to spring him.

Amos and the Vampire

It's Halloween and Amos Binder's big sister, Amy, has a date with a real freak. She's always dating rejects, but this guy looks like he was rejected by the grave! He's got pale skin, dark hair, mesmerizing eyes, and an annoying tendency to disappear, and he wants to have the Binders over for a late-night Halloween snack. . . . Can Amos and Dunc stop the vampire before he starts to bite? Or will Amy and her man do a little necking she will never forget?

Amos and the Chameleon Caper

She's a master of disguises—able to change identities at will. She's wanted in five states. They call her the Chameleon. Dunc thinks he and Amos are just about to crack the case wide open. All they have to do is sneak into this dangerous felon's apartment!